Daisy the Doughnut Fairy

Tim Bugbird · Lara Ede

make
believe
ideas

Once upon an island
in the deep, blue sea,
lived a mermaid fairy family –
Daisy, Dolly and Dee.

Days were filled with fun
as the fairies swam and flew,
but apart from making doughnuts,
there wasn't much to do!

Doughnut
Island

Their **fairy** wands made every kind –
hundreds by the hour!

But the doughnut mountains grew and grew
'til there was **no room** in their tower.

So Daisy called a meeting of her fairy clan.
They put their heads together – what they needed was a plan!

Daisy, Dee and Dolly thought hard for hours and hours.
Finding uses for the doughnuts used up all their fairy powers!

Wheels

The **first** idea was Dolly's —
it didn't work as she wihed:
the **wheels** looked
good enough to eat
but soon got very **squihed**!

Earrings

This was Dee's **best** idea,
but she didn't think it through –
they were far **too big** to dangle
and the *frosting*
stuck like glue!

Sunglasses

The **third** idea was Daisy's. At first it seemed quite good, but **glasses** made from doughnuts just don't work the way they should!

It was nothing
less than awful –
there was nothing
left to try.

At least that's what the fairies thought, until a pirate ship sailed by.

Pancake Pete was **all aboard**
   with first mate Fearsome Fred,
but neither one could see the **rocks**
   for the **pancakes** on their heads!

They splished and sploshed and splashed and splished, until they turned bright pink!

Peering through the window
and thinking very fast,
Daisy said, "I think we have
a use for these at last!"

Doughnut Island

She took some doughnuts from the pile
and threw them to the boat.
The pirates jumped inside the rings –
they really helped them float!

The Pancake Pirates **bobbed** to shore,

their timbers all a-shiver.

Dee and Dolly felt quite scared,
and Daisy began to quiver.

and sailing doughnut dinghies

was the most fun

we've ever had!"

The Pirates were so grateful, and asked,

"What can we do?"

Daisy said,

"There's a job for us

in sea search and rescue!"

So the fairies and the pirates learned how to work together,
helping folk in trouble at sea or lost in stormy weather.

Every day was an adventure,
hard work but full of fun,
and their doughnuts
had a use at last –
every single one!

So that's how Daisy's doughnuts stopped the pirates sinking and a mermaid fairy saved the day with true friends and quick thinking!